DC SUPER HEROES

THE DARK KNIGHT ™

DANGER ON DECK!

WRITTEN BY
SCOTT SONNEBORN

ILLUSTRATED BY
LUCIANO VECCHIO

BATMAN CREATED BY BOB KANE
WITH BILL FINGER

RAINTREE IS AN IMPRINT OF CAPSTONE GLOBAL LIBRARY LIMITED, A COMPANY INCORPORATED IN ENGLAND AND WALES HAVING ITS REGISTERED OFFICE AT 264 BANBURY ROAD, OXFORD, OX2 7DY – REGISTERED COMPANY NUMBER: 6695582

WWW.RAINTREE.CO.UK
MYORDERS@RAINTREE.CO.UK

ISBN 978 1 4747 3295 6
21 20 19 18 17
10 9 8 7 6 5 4 3 2 1

BRITISH LIBRARY CATALOGUING IN PUBLICATION DATA
A FULL CATALOGUE RECORD FOR THIS BOOK IS AVAILABLE FROM THE BRITISH LIBRARY.

PRINTED AND BOUND IN CHINA

CONTENTS

WHILE STILL A BOY, BRUCE WAYNE WITNESSED THE BRUTAL MURDER OF HIS PARENTS. THIS TRAGIC EVENT CHANGED THE YOUNG BILLIONAIRE FOREVER. BRUCE VOWED TO RID GOTHAM CITY OF EVIL, AND KEEP ITS PEOPLE SAFE FROM CRIME. AFTER YEARS OF TRAINING HIS BODY AND MIND, HE DONNED A NEW UNIFORM AND A NEW IDENTITY.

HE BECAME...

THE DARK KNIGHT

CHAPTER 1

ALL ABOARD!

VRRROOOOOOOOOOOOOOOOOOOOM!

The Batmobile roared through the last moments of the night. As the sun rose over Gotham City, Batman drove through the secret entrance of the Batcave and came to a screeching stop.

Batman took off his mask, revealing the weary face of Bruce Wayne underneath. Bruce was exhausted after a long night of fighting crime. All he wanted was to drag himself into bed for a full day of sleep.

So, Bruce was very disappointed to find himself, thirty minutes later, in the back of a limousine. His loyal butler, Alfred Pennyworth, was at the wheel.

"I don't know how you talked me into doing this," complained Bruce. He looked down at the flowery Hawaiian shirt, shorts and flip-flops he was wearing. "And why did you insist I wear these ridiculous clothes?"

"You are wearing the proper costume for the circumstances," replied the butler. "If it were the middle of the night and you were about to face the Joker, then I would have laid out the Batsuit for you."

Alfred turned the steering wheel and pulled the limo into a parking space at the Gotham City Docks.

"Right now, however, it is daytime," Alfred continued, "and we are about to board a cruise ship."

Bruce rubbed the corners of his eyes with his fingers. "Explain to me again why I'm going on this charity cruise," he asked.

"The fifty richest people in Gotham are going to be aboard this ship," the butler replied. "If Bruce Wayne doesn't do the things a typical billionaire does, people might start asking questions. The kind of questions someone who has a secret Batcave under his house doesn't need."

Bruce sighed. He knew Alfred was right.

When it came to being Batman, Bruce always knew what to do. But when it came to being billionaire Bruce Wayne, he would have been lost without Alfred's guidance.

Bruce also knew the cruise was raising money for a charity. Just as important, the ship would only be at sea for the day. Bruce would be back at Gotham Harbour by nightfall, just in time for him to go to work – as Batman.

The only thing he was going to miss was a good day's sleep.

As he walked up the gangplank to the ship, Bruce saw that the outside of the hull was a smoothly polished white. The captain was there, pointing out the vines that decorated the boat's banisters and railings. "That's a depiction of the endangered plant that this charity cruise is trying to save," he explained.

Alfred led Bruce up the gangplank, wheeling the four huge suitcases he had packed for his employer.

Stacked on top of each other, the suitcases reached the butler's neck.

"Here, let me help you," said Bruce as he grabbed two of the cases. "Do I even need all this? We're only going to be gone for a few hours."

"Good packing is the secret to any successful trip, no matter how long it lasts," replied Alfred. He pointed to the other passengers. Each of them had half a dozen suitcases and trunks as well. Some of them had many more than that.

"If a billionaire had arrived without several changes of clothes," said Alfred, "they would have stuck out like a sore thumb."

When everyone was on board, the ship pulled out of Gotham Harbour.

As the ship cut quietly through the waves, the passengers lounged on deckchairs by the pool or in the shade of the nearby lifeboats. Everyone was enjoying themselves by eating hors d'oeuvres, drinking champagne and chatting.

Everyone except Bruce.

Most people would feel miserable if they were out in the middle of a cold and windy Gotham City night. That's where Bruce felt most at home, stalking from shadow to shadow in pursuit of his prey. Now, sitting in the sun in his Hawaiian shirt and flip-flops, Bruce felt completely out of his element.

"Oh, wipe that sour look off your face, Brucie!" squealed Dolores Fitzpatrick. She sat down in the lounge chair next to Bruce.

"This is fabulous!" Dolores continued. She snapped her fingers impatiently in the air. "At least, it would be if I could get any service around here. Waiter? WAITER!"

Mrs Fitzpatrick was one of the richest women in Gotham. She was also one of the largest. Some people said that her mouth was pretty big, too. Judging by the volume of her scream, Bruce had to say she was living up to expectations so far.

"Over here! Chop-chop!" she shouted at a nearby crew member. "Can't you see this giant flower thingy is blocking my sun!"

Mrs Fitzpatrick was pointing at the enormous display of flowers and vines in the middle of the deck. It looked like a statue of a beautiful woman, but it was crafted entirely out of vines and flowers.

The plant statue cast a large shadow over the deck of the boat. A tiny part of which fell over Mrs Fitzpatrick's little toe.

"I'm very sorry, Mrs Fitzpatrick," a tall crew member said politely. "I'll have it moved right away!"

The man signalled to the rest of the crew members to help him move the enormous display of flowers and vines. It looked to Bruce that it was just as heavy as it was complex. Even the captain came over to help. As they struggled to move the statue, it shook.

WOOOOOOOOSH!

Suddenly, pollen flew out and covered the captain and crew.

Mrs Fitzpatrick didn't seem concerned about all the fuss she was causing.

"I know there are only a handful of crew members working at this special charity cruise," Dolores said to Bruce without looking at him, "but don't you think they could do a better job? The service is terrible!"

Bruce thought they were doing a more than adequate job of serving the impossible Mrs Fitzpatrick. But before he could answer, a harsh voice called out to all the passengers.

"All of you get up! Move!" the tall crew member shouted. "Go to your cabins right now!"

Bruce was shocked to see the other crew members join him in grabbing Mrs Fitzpatrick and the other passengers and pushing them towards the cabins.

"Why, of all the nerve!" Mrs Fitzpatrick shouted. "One does not shove a Fitzpatrick! Especially if one is a servant! I am here to be charitable and expect shoddy service, but this is just too rude!"

"There, there, now," cooed a sultry woman's voice. "Don't be mad at him. It's not his fault. He's just not himself at the moment. In fact, right now, he's mine!"

Bruce turned to see who had spoken. He was surprised to hear that the voice somehow came from inside the plant statue.

The statue's petals and leaves unfolded and fell away. Vines unwound and dropped to the floor. Now Bruce could see that it wasn't a statue at all. The plants had just been there to cover a woman hidden underneath.

"Now every person in the crew is under my control," said the woman. "Thanks to this special pollen."

As soon as Bruce saw the woman's bright red hair, pale green skin and deadly smile, he knew instantly who it was.

Poison Ivy.

CHAPTER 2

THE POISON PLOT

"Unfortunately," Poison Ivy told the shocked and frightened passengers, "I don't have enough pollen to control all of you, too. But I think my crew members can handle that for me."

The crew members moved to herd the passengers. Bruce grabbed Alfred and ran the other way. Ivy waved a hand. A tangle of vines leaped off a railing and snaked around Bruce and Alfred, holding them in place.

"Oops," Ivy said with a smile. "Did I forget to mention that I can command any plant to do what I want? In other words, that means all the vines decorating this ship also work for me."

"Oh, I know all about you, Poison Ivy!" Bruce shouted as he struggled against the vines.

Then Bruce stopped. For a moment, he had almost forgotten he wasn't in costume. "I've read a lot about you in the newspapers," he finished quickly. "You're always bad news."

Alfred shot Bruce a relieved look. Things were already bad enough. If Poison Ivy discovered that Bruce Wayne was secretly Batman, there's no telling how much worse the situation might get.

Ivy smiled at Bruce. "Well isn't that flattering," she said. "Gotham's richest, most eligible bachelor knows my name." She placed her hand to her forehead and pretended to swoon.

She dropped her hand, and her smile quickly dropped into a scowl. "But I hate newspapers!" she said. "They cut down beautiful trees to make them. As far as I'm concerned, the world would be a better place without newspapers – and the people who read them!"

Bruce had much more to say to her, but he averted his eyes and bit his tongue. He had to continue to play the role of the scared billionaire – not the World's Greatest Detective.

"But – but this is a charity event," spluttered Dolores Fitzpatrick.

"And the proceeds are going towards saving a very rare flower!" Dolores continued. "I thought you were supposed to be some kind of plant lover. Doesn't this charity help your cause?"

"Why save just one type of flower when you can save them all?" replied Ivy. "So many rich people in one place at one time was simply too tempting a target. When I ransom each and every one of you, I'll have all the money I need to protect all the plants in the hemisphere – not just one!"

Ivy pushed back her red hair with her hand. "Until then," she said with a coy smile, "you are my hostages."

Ivy's vines dragged Bruce and Alfred away. The mesmerized crew members herded the other passengers.

Ivy's hostages were led down several decks, then shoved into their respective cabins.

"If the crew members under my control catch someone trying to leave their cabin," Ivy shouted, "they will go to the next cabin and throw whoever is inside over the edge of the ship. And they will continue throwing people overboard until whoever left their cabin returns. So don't even try to escape!"

Ivy ordered the crew members to lock all the doors and stand guard outside them in the corridor. Then she turned to face the captain. "Now, you and I have some business to discuss," said Ivy. "Meet me on the bridge."

Under her spell, the captain nodded and followed.

The rest of the hypnotized crew stayed in the corridor. They stood guard like zombie sailors.

"Can't get out that way," Bruce said to himself, inspecting the door. "Not without putting other passengers in danger."

Bruce looked around for another way to escape. Other than the door to the corridor, the only exit led to a small outdoor balcony. Bruce slid the glass door open and stepped out into the cool ocean breeze.

Bruce looked up. The deck above was a few metres away. Between his balcony and that deck, the ship's slick hull was far too smooth to climb.

If Alfred had let Bruce bring his grapnel gun and the rest of the equipment in his Utility Belt, he could have made the climb.

However, with only his bare hands and flip-flops, the task would be impossible. The other deck might as well have been a thousand metres away.

"Ok, I can't climb up," Bruce told himself. "So where can I go?"

To Bruce's right was a balcony identical to his own. It was only a few metres away. *No problem for someone who spends his nights jumping from rooftop to rooftop chasing criminals*, thought Bruce.

Bruce leaped. **THUMP!** He landed on the balcony next door. Then, carefully, he slid open the glass door to the cabin and stepped inside from the balcony.

"I say!" shouted the occupant of the cabin. "Who do you think you are – oh, it's you!"

Bruce smiled. The cabin belonged to Alfred. "How did you know I'd be here, sir?" the butler asked.

"I had a feeling my butler would have been assigned the cabin next to mine," Bruce told him.

"I assume you have a plan to deal with our present . . . situation?" asked Alfred.

"I'm working on it," said Bruce. "I need to get up to the bridge. I don't dare go out through the cabin door and put any of the other passengers at risk. But the hull outside is too slick to climb with my bare hands."

Alfred nodded. "I see."

"And even if I could get up there," Bruce added, "I don't have any of my tools or weapons."

"And since Ivy has the whole crew under her spell," Alfred added, "You'd be unarmed, and outnumbered twenty to one."

Bruce flopped down on the bed. "If I just had the Batmobile or my Utility Belt," he told Alfred, "I'd feel a lot better about our chances."

"Unfortunately, sir, it was impossible to pack the Batmobile," the butler said dryly. "However . . ."

Alfred touched a hidden button on one of the larger suitcases. The secret compartment opened up to reveal Bruce's Batman uniform!

CLICK! CLICK! CLICK! The butler pressed the hidden buttons on the rest of the luggage.

Each piece of luggage held some of Batman's crime-fighting tools and weapons.

"As I always say," said Alfred, "proper packing is the most important part of any trip."

"And like *I* always say," replied Bruce, "I don't know what I'd do without you, Alfred."

Alfred nodded. "Neither do I," he said, handing Bruce his costume.

Bruce quickly put on his Batman costume and strapped his Utility Belt around his waist. Then he stepped onto the balcony outside Alfred's cabin.

The Dark Knight looked up. The deck above was just as far away as before. But this time, Batman had his Utility Belt – and his grapnel gun!

Batman aimed the gun and pulled the trigger. **THWIP!** A cable darted up through the air. **CLANK!** The hook at the cable's end slipped around the railing on the deck above. Batman pulled the cable tight and began to climb quickly.

When he reached the next deck, it was empty. All of the passengers were imprisoned on the deck below. That's where the whole crew was as well, standing guard as Ivy had commanded. Only the captain had gone with Ivy up to the bridge. The rest of the ship was completely empty.

As Batman climbed up the hull towards the bridge, he peered into the decks he passed and made note of his surroundings. He saw the cruise liner had a ballroom, a bowling alley and a cinema.

When he reached the top, he saw that the ship also had the most high-tech bridge of any cruise ship on the planet. On most ships, the bridge is where the captain pilots the boat. On this ship, the bridge was so technologically advanced that the vessel practically steered itself, which was a good thing – because, like the rest of his crew, the captain was under the spell of Ivy's mind-controlling pollen. He could do only what Ivy ordered him to do, and Ivy had commanded him to keep all his attention on the ship's radar.

The radar could pick up any nearby planes or boats. If the Gotham City Police tried to stop Ivy, she'd see them coming. Which, at that moment, is exactly what Ivy was telling Police Commissioner Gordon over the ship's radio.

Batman listened to the conversation from a railing some distance away, through the radio receiver in his cowl. The high-tech receiver had been designed to pick up any police transmission. Batman was glad it still worked this far out at sea.

"Listen to me, Ivy," Batman heard Commissioner Gordon reply over the radio. "I need to know you won't hurt anyone on board!"

"Oh, I won't hurt anyone on board," said Ivy. "Because I'll throw everyone overboard! The moment the captain sees anything approaching on the radar, I will make every last one of the passengers walk the plank into the sea where I'll leave them to drown!"

Batman grimaced. He knew Ivy well enough to believe her threat.

Ivy wanted every plant on Earth to be loved and protected, but she couldn't care less what happened to people.

"I understand, Ivy," Commissioner Gordon said over the radio. "We won't go near the ship. I promise."

Batman knew Gordon would keep his word. No help would be coming from the police. Saving everyone on board was up to the Dark Knight.

Batman looked up. The bridge was still far above him. **PHWISSSH!** He fired his grapnel gun.

KA-THUNK!

Its hook grabbed hold of a railing. Batman jumped off his perch and swung towards the bridge.

SQUAWKKKKKKKKKKKKK!

The radio in Batman's cowl crackled to life. "There's something on the radar!" shouted the captain. "It wasn't there a second ago, but now the object is approaching fast!"

"It's not us!" replied Commissioner Gordon over the police radio. "I swear to you, it's not the police!"

As he swung in mid-air, a chill went down Batman's spine. Had the radar spotted him?

"I don't believe it!" stammered the captain. "It's . . ."

Batman saw it the same moment the captain said it. "It's an iceberg!" the captain cried.

And the ship was about to crash right into it!

Swinging out over the open air, there was nothing Batman could do.

RUMBLE!

The front of the ship smashed into the giant hunk of floating ice.

CRRREEEEEEEEK!

RUMMMMMMMMBLE!

The entire boat shook. Batman lost his grip on his cable and fell down to the deck below.

WHAM!

He landed hard on the railing, then tumbled over the side of the boat.

Batman slid down the slick hull of the ship.

SKREEEEEEEEEEEEEEE!

There was nothing to grab hold of. The slippery metal hull slid beneath his fingers as he fell straight down towards the sea.

CHAPTER 3

ON ICE

As he fell, Batman flipped open a pouch on his Utility Belt and unfolded one of the Batarangs inside. Just as he was about to hit the water, Batman pressed a button on the Batarang. **WHIRRRRRRRRRR!** A tiny electromagnet inside it hummed to life.

THUNK! Batman clamped the magnetic Batarang onto the ship's metal hull. It held fast. Batman dangled from it by one arm, just above the water.

This doesn't make sense, thought Batman as he caught his breath. *The water off the coast of Gotham City is far too warm for an iceberg, especially in the summer. So why does it look like that hunk of ice is getting bigger?*

Hanging from the side of the ship, Batman watched the iceberg slowly rise higher and higher – right up to the bridge on the top deck of the ship.

Then Batman saw that a man in a metal suit was riding on top of the ice. The man was making the iceberg larger and larger by freezing the ocean water with a futuristic-looking gun.

"Of course!" Batman realized as he recognized the man. "An iceberg in the middle of summer has to be the work of Mr Freeze!"

Standing on the very top of the iceberg, Mr Freeze didn't notice Batman was hiding below. Instead, he lifted his weapon and focused his aim on the bridge.

ZAP! He fired his freeze gun. Instantly, the bridge's wrap-around window shattered with a *CRASH!*

ZAP! Another blast from the cold gun created a slide from the iceberg to the bridge. *SWISSH!* Mr Freeze slid down the ice chute and into the ship, disappearing from Batman's sight.

"I've got to get up there," Batman said to himself. "It's only a matter of time before Ivy and Mr Freeze find each other."

Batman fired his grapnel gun. The hook hit the slippery metal hull and fell back down. It landed in the water with a *SPLASH!*

Batman pulled up the hook, but there was no use trying to fire it again. There was nothing within reach for it to latch onto. He was stuck. All he could do was listen through his earpiece.

"What did the ship hit?" asked Commissioner Gordon over the radio. "Don't do anything rash, Ivy! Just tell us what you want!"

On the bridge, Mr Freeze grabbed the radio handset.

"What Poison Ivy wants is no longer important," said the frosty villain. "You will only get the hostages if you agree to *my* demands."

"Mr Freeze?!" exclaimed Gordon over the radio. "I don't understand! Who exactly is hijacking this ship?"

"That's an excellent question, Commissioner," cooed Ivy.

Batman heard the entire conversation over the police radio as he hung from his magnetic Batarang. Suddenly, another voice broke in over the radio with a **SQUAWK** of static.

"Sir, I hope this isn't a bad moment to interrupt," Alfred's voice crackled over the cowl's built-in radio. "But whatever we just crashed into seems to have Ivy's mesmerized crew members worried. They are now going cabin to cabin to make sure all the hostages are where they should be. Looking through the peephole in my cabin door, I can't help but notice that very shortly they will arrive at your cabin."

Bruce's eyes went wide beneath his mask.

"If they find it empty –" Batman began.

"They will throw the person in the next cabin overboard," finished the butler in a steady voice. "And, unfortunately, it seems that person would be me."

Bruce knew he had to get back to his cabin and fast. But there was nothing his grapnel hook could attach to. The only thing within reach was the slick surface of the hull. And the only thing he had that would stick to that was the magnetic Batarang he was hanging from.

"So that's what I'll have to use," Batman decided. **CLINK!** He activated the release switch on the magnet and pulled it off the hull. Immediately, he started to fall. As he was about to drop into the ocean, he attached the magnet to the end of his grapnel gun.

SPLASH!

Batman hit the water hard. As he plunged under the waves, he fired his grapnel gun upwards. **FWIP!** The cable shot up out of the water with the magnet on its end. **CLUNK!**

The magnet hit the side of the boat and held fast. Batman pulled himself out of the water and climbed up the cable.

"The easy part is over," Batman said. "Now I have to get back to my cabin in time!"

Hand over hand, Batman scaled the long grapnel hook rope as fast as he could. His muscles soon began to ache with the effort, but he kept climbing. Less than two minutes later, Batman landed on the balcony outside his cabin with a resounding **THUMP!**

But he was too late. Through the sliding glass door, Bruce saw a crew member was already in his cabin.

CHAPTER 4

COLD HEARTS

Dripping wet, Batman quickly ducked down and hid on the balcony. Beyond the crew member in his cabin, Batman could see that the door to the corridor was open. Bruce saw several more crew members standing out in the corridor. All of them carried walkie-talkies.

"There may be more crew members I can't see," worried Batman. "If I take these down, the others might sound an alarm or call Ivy."

Batman ducked lower on the balcony so the crew member couldn't see him through the glass door. As he tried to work out what to do next, he saw Alfred step out of the cabin's bathroom.

"I say!" Alfred said to the crew member in the cabin. "What are you doing in my cabin?"

"We're checking all the cabins to make sure everyone's where they're supposed to be," said the mesmerized crew member. He held up a clipboard. It listed the passengers' names and their cabin numbers on it.

"It says here that this is supposed to be Bruce Wayne's cabin," the crew member said. He jabbed his thumb at Alfred. "You had better explain why you're in it."

"There must be some mistake," replied Alfred. "This is my cabin. I am Mr Bruce Wayne's manservant. My employer is next door."

"We'll see about that," said the crew member. He signalled to another crew member in the corridor to check the cabin next door.

Out on the balcony, Batman leaped up from where he was hiding and jumped over to the balcony next door. As he slid into the empty cabin, he looked at the door to the corridor. **CREAK!** The doorknob started to turn.

THUMP! A crew member threw open the door. He looked around the cabin and found Bruce Wayne in the bed underneath the covers.

"Any trouble?" Bruce asked the crew member.

The crew member just grunted and went back into the corridor. "Bruce Wayne is in this cabin," he shouted to the other mesmerized crew members. "That butler was telling the truth."

As soon as the crew member shut the door behind him, Bruce flung off the sheets. He was still wearing his soaked Batman costume underneath. He had only had time to take off his mask before the crew member had entered.

Batman put his mask back on and slipped back over to the other balcony. He saw that Alfred was alone and that the door to the corridor was closed.

Batman slipped into the cabin.

"Good to see you again, sir," said Alfred. "I am very glad that worked."

"Me too," Bruce told his butler. "How did you get here from your cabin with all those crew members in the corridor?"

"The same way you did," replied Alfred. "Over the balcony."

Bruce's eyes went wide. "You jumped?" he asked in surprise.

The butler sighed. He gingerly rubbed his sore knees and elbows. "Indeed," he said. "I know that the situation is dire with Poison Ivy on board, but you'll forgive me if I say that I'm in no hurry to do that again."

"It's not just Ivy," said Batman. "Mr Freeze is here now, too. We've got to get all the passengers off this ship."

Bruce saw a worried look cross Alfred's face. "But don't worry," Bruce reassured him. "Mrs Fitzpatrick and many of the other passengers couldn't climb over their balconies even once."

"That much is true," Alfred said. "That means we're going to have to find some way to get them past those crew members in the corridor."

* * *

On the bridge, the ship's intercom rang out with a loud **CRACKLE!**

"All the hostages are in their cabins," a crew member announced through the intercom.

"That's nice," said Ivy, glancing at Mr Freeze, "but I've got bigger cold fish to fry at the moment."

"Indeed you do," said Mr Freeze. "It appears we both had the same idea to hijack this ship, which is logical. The fifty richest people in Gotham are on board – and far from the police or Batman. Taking them hostage was a very clever, rational plan."

Ivy smiled. "Thank you," she said.

Mr Freeze aimed his freeze gun at her. "However," he stated coldly, "only one of us can ransom the hostages for what we want."

"Oh, I don't know about that," Ivy said calmly. "You may be an uninvited guest, but that doesn't mean my party has to end."

Poison Ivy crept closer to Freeze. She smiled coyly at him.

"In fact, you're exactly the kind of man I like to have around. Tall, pale and heavily armed," Ivy added, pointing at Mr Freeze's cold gun.

"If you are attempting to get me to like you," Mr Freeze said coldly, "you should know that plan won't work. All my feelings have been locked away in cold storage. I care nothing about you, nor anyone else on this hunk of metal."

Ivy shrugged. "Okay, so I was right – you are a cold fish," she said, rolling her eyes. "But we can still do this together. You can be my partner."

Ivy slinked closer. "Well, maybe not exactly my partner," she whispered. "More like my slave!"

WOOOOOOOSH!

Ivy blew a handful of pollen at Mr Freeze. The pollen entered his respiratory apparatus and passed into his helmet.

"That's the same mind-controlling pollen I used on the captain and the crew," Poison Ivy said. "I don't have enough to use on all the passengers, but I have just enough left for you. I think you'll find its effects are instantaneous!"

"Perhaps I would," replied Mr Freeze. "If it could get through my cold-sealed suit. Unfortunately for you, neither heat nor air – nor your precious pollen – can do that. My filters have already nullified your pixie dust."

THUMP! Mr Freeze shoved Ivy away. "So do not think you can do to me what you did to this ship's crew," he said.

"Perhaps I can't," snarled Ivy, "for now. But let's see what happens when I crack that suit open!"

Mr Freeze didn't seem concerned. "I doubt you will be able to do that," said Mr Freeze. "It would take an entire army to force open my suit's pressurized titanium seals."

Ivy simply smiled at Mr Freeze. "Well, I may not have an army of soldiers," she replied. "But I do have plenty of mindless sailors!"

Ivy lunged and hit the intercom button on the wall.

CLICK!

"Attention all crew members!" she shouted into the intercom. "Get up here and put Mr Freeze on ice!"

SQUAWK! SQUAWK!

Down on the passenger deck, the crew members heard the announcement through their walkie-talkies. They all nodded and ran towards the stairs.

Batman peeked through the peephole in the cabin door. He saw the crew members leaving.

"Looks like it's time to go!" said Batman as he started taking off his costume.

Alfred was surprised. "Sir, if you're going into action," asked Alfred, "won't you be needing your costume?"

"You're half right," Bruce said, "but it has to be the right costume for the occasion." Bruce slipped into his Hawaiian shirt and flip-flops.

Alfred gave Bruce a confused look.

"None of the passengers has met Batman before," Bruce explained. "They might be as scared of him as they are of Ivy and Mr Freeze. But they do know Bruce Wayne and his butler."

Alfred smiled. "I never thought I'd see the day you'd choose a Hawaiian shirt over your cape and cowl," said Alfred.

KNOCK! KNOCK!

Out in the corridor, Bruce and Alfred knocked on the door of every cabin. They told the other passengers that this was their chance to escape. Bruce said he had seen lifeboats near the pool. He insisted everyone follow him to them now.

At first, the passengers started to follow Bruce and Alfred.

That is, until Mrs Fitzpatrick's voice suddenly boomed out. "I will do no such thing!" she said. "I will not leave all my belongings behind. I need time to pack my things!"

Alfred politely reminded her that this was their only chance to escape the ship. Mrs Fitzpatrick cut him off as soon as he began.

"Nobody tells a Fitzpatrick what to do!" she growled. "Especially some stuffy butler! I've had quite enough of being ordered around. I'm not going anywhere until all my bags are packed!"

The rest of the wealthy passengers started to hesitate. Hearing Dolores Fitzpatrick's complaints seemed to weaken their resolve to escape.

Bruce shot Alfred a look. They didn't have time for this. Dolores needed to be silenced, and quickly.

But how? wondered Bruce.

CHAPTER 5

SHATTERED PLANS

Up on the bridge, Mr Freeze blasted at Ivy.

ZIRRRRT!

Ivy waved a hand and made the plants in front of her grow tall enough to block the blast. Covered in ice, the plants turned brittle and crumbled.

"I'm so sorry, darlings," Ivy whispered to the frozen plants, "but it was you or me!"

CRASH!

Glass shattered as Ivy jumped through the window.

SPLOOSH! She landed with a splash in the pool on the deck below.

Mr Freeze quickly leaped down to the pool deck.

"Put Mr Freeze on ice, Captain!" ordered Ivy as she pulled herself out of the pool.

Under Ivy's spell, the captain had no choice but to obey. He jumped down from the bridge at Mr Freeze. He was still in the air when the villain fired his gun.

FWAZIP! A sub-zero blast turned the captain into a frozen statue that hit the deck with a **CLUNK!**

"Was that supposed to impress me?" asked Mr Freeze.

"No," Ivy said with a smile. "It was supposed to distract you!"

Ivy pointed over Mr Freeze's shoulder. The rest of the crew had arrived. **WHAM! WHAM! WHAM!** They all pounced on Mr Freeze, slamming him with their fists.

Ivy smiled as she watched the crew hammer Mr Freeze with punch after punch. But her smile disappeared when she saw that none of the blows hurt Mr Freeze at all. He was perfectly safe inside his armoured suit.

WHOOMP! Mr Freeze threw the crew members off him, then raised his gun. **ZAP! ZAP! ZAP!** He froze them all into statues.

"Were these all of the crew members under your control?" asked Mr Freeze.

"That was every last one of them, and it wasn't nearly enough to stop you," admitted Ivy. "Still, you can't blame a girl for trying."

"No," said Mr Freeze coldly, "but I can blame you for ordering all the crew members up here. If they are here, who is guarding the passengers?"

Ivy's eyes went wide. "No one," she whispered. "I was too busy worrying about you!"

"Perhaps the most logical course would be for us to put aside our differences for the moment," said Mr Freeze. "If the passengers escape, neither of us will get anything."

"I think we've finally found something we can agree on," said Ivy.

Ivy and Mr Freeze turned towards the door that led to the passenger deck . . . only to find Batman blocking their path!

"You're here too?!" cried Ivy. "Is there anyone who wears a costume in Gotham who's *not* on this ship?"

"We are going down to check on the passengers," Mr Freeze said to Batman. "Step aside or be destroyed."

"We may not be in Gotham City," replied Batman, "but these passengers are Gotham citizens. Which means they're under my protection."

"Enough discussion," said Mr Freeze.

ZIRRRRRRT! He fired his cold gun, but Batman was already running. The blast missed him and hit the ship's swimming pool instead.

CRACKLE! Instantly, every drop of water in the pool turned to ice!

With the frozen water expanding, the ice was now too big to fit in the pool. **CRUNCH!** It smashed through the bottom of the pool and landed in the ship's bowling alley on the deck below.

WHAM!

Batman rammed his shoulder into Mr Freeze and Ivy, pushing them down through the hole where the pool had been.

The three tumbled down onto the ruined bowling alley. Upon landing, they all quickly sprang away from each other.

Ivy raised her hands. "Get out of our way!" she screamed. The vines decorating the bowling alley came to life and surged straight at the Dark Knight.

He ducked just in time. **CRUNCH!** The vines smashed through a window behind him.

Batman braced for another attack. But Ivy suddenly stopped, her mouth falling open in surprise.

"Look!" she cried to Mr Freeze.

Through the broken window of the bowling alley, the villains saw a group of lifeboats floating away from them. Not only had Alfred got all the passengers into the lifeboats – he had got all their luggage on, as well!

Alfred was tending to the captain and the other frozen crew members in one of the lifeboats. They would be fine in a few hours, Batman knew, after they thawed out and the effects of Ivy's pollen had worn off.

"It's over," Batman told Ivy and Mr Freeze.

Mr Freeze nodded coolly. "Obviously, Poison Ivy and I cannot ransom hostages we no longer have," he said. "But there is one thing we can still accomplish that would be even more valuable to our criminal careers."

Ivy sneered at Batman. "Yes," she said. "We'll make sure Batman goes down with this ship!"

Ivy waved her hands again. Suddenly, every vine and plant on the ship squirmed to life and grabbed hold of a railing, banister or porthole.

"Pull!" she commanded.

All across the boat, the plants tore at the ship.

CREAK! A crack rippled across the ship's hull. Water surged into the lower decks. The ship was sinking!

"Stop!" yelled Batman. He lunged at Ivy. She waved her hands and a thicket of vines wrapped around Batman's legs. They lifted him up and slammed him into the ground with a thundering **THUD!!**

Mr Freeze stepped up and fired at Batman. **ZIRRRRRRT!** Batman rolled to his side. The sub-zero blast hit the vines instead. **CLANK!** The vines froze instantly. A hard kick from Batman broke them off with a **SNAP!**

Batman sprang to his feet and threw a Batarang that sailed just past Ivy. The Batarang sliced into a rack on the wall of the bowling alley. **CLANK!**

"Ha! You missed!" Ivy snarled.

Batman smirked. "Did I?" he asked.

Suddenly, the twelve bowling balls on the rack bounced free.

THUMP! THUMP! THUMP!

Batman jumped aside as they slammed into the villains. Mr Freeze fell to the floor along with Poison Ivy.

Ivy was knocked unconscious. Mr Freeze, however, quickly got to his feet, unharmed because of his armoured suit. "You will have to do better than that to stop me," said Mr Freeze.

Suddenly, the massive ship started to slide beneath the waves. Water rushed into the room.

SPLOOOSH!

In an instant, the water was nearly knee-deep – and rising fast.

Mr Freeze rushed at Batman through the water. *ZIRRRRRT!* Mr Freeze fired his gun, but Batman rolled like a gymnast to avoid the blast.

"You can't keep dodging my blasts forever," said Mr Freeze as the water continued to rise higher.

"You're right," Batman said.

As the villain fired again, Batman tackled Mr Freeze. *WHAM!* Mr Freeze's blast went off course as he fell over into the waist-deep water.

Batman leaped to his feet just as Mr Freeze's errant blast hit the water. Instantly, every drop of water in the room froze into rock-solid ice.

Mr Freeze found himself encased in a thousand-tonne block of solid ice! He couldn't even move an arm to try to break free.

Batman breathed a sigh of relief – but then he saw that one of his feet was also trapped in the ice! As the water rose above his chest, Batman pulled as hard as he could. His foot moved a little, but didn't come free.

With a resounding **SPLOOOOOOOOSH**, the boat sank beneath the waves. In a matter of seconds, the entire ship had disappeared into the dark . . . taking Batman along with it.

* * *

An hour later on the Gotham Docks, Alfred helped the other passengers out of the lifeboats.

The sun was going down, but he kept looking out at the water, hoping to see any sign of Batman.

Instead, he saw two figures coming closer to the shore. Alfred was alarmed to see that the two were Ivy and Mr Freeze!

Alfred worried about what they had done to Batman. Until he saw that the two villains were unconscious. A third person, in black clothes almost too dark to see, was swimming ahead and dragging the other two.

Batman!

As the weary hero climbed up onto a dark and empty dock near by, Alfred quickly rushed over without anyone noticing. He arrived just as Batman finished tying up the unconscious villains.

"It's good to see you, sir," said Alfred, barely restraining his glee. "I must apologize, the cruise was not exactly what I was expecting."

"Me neither," replied Batman. "It actually worked out a lot *better* than I had expected."

"It did?" asked Alfred.

"If we hadn't been on that boat, I doubt all the passengers and crew would have made it back safely," said Batman.

Aflred nodded. "Quite true," he said.

As the moon rose over Gotham, a police siren began to wail in the distance. "And we got back in time for me to go to work," he said.

Batman raised his grapnel gun and fired a cable into the air. *WOOOOOOOSH!*

"So all in all, the next time you suggest we go on something like this," Batman told Alfred, "remind me not to complain."

Alfred smiled and waved goodbye. With that, Batman disappeared into the night.

POISON IVY

REAL NAME:
Pamela Isley

OCCUPATION:
Professional criminal,
Botanist

BASE:
Gotham City

HEIGHT:
1.67 metres

WEIGHT:
50 kilograms

EYES:
Green

HAIR:
Red

Born with immunities to plant toxins and poisons,
Pamela Isley's love of plants began to grow like a weed
at an early age. She eventually became a botanist (plant
scientist). Through reckless experimentation with various
flora, Pamela Isley's skin itself has become poisonous.
Her venomous lips and poisonous plant weapons present
a real problem for the Dark Knight. But Ivy's most
dangerous quality is her extreme love of nature – she
cares more about the smallest seed than any human life.

MR FREEZE

REAL NAME:
Dr Victor Fries

OCCUPATION:
Professional criminal,
Scientist

BASE:
Gotham City

HEIGHT:
1.82 metres

WEIGHT:
88 kilograms

EYES:
Icy blue

HAIR:
None

Victor Fries felt lonely throughout his schooling. He was teased constantly by classmates and was sure he'd never have a friend. Then he met Nora, and everything changed. They fell in love. But when Nora became ill with an incurable disease, Victor lost hope. To say Victor's heart went cold would be an understatement. His indifference towards human life is now so severe that he spreads suffering to anyone within his icy grasp. That way, other people will feel his pain.

BIOGRAPHIES

SCOTT SONNEBORN has written many books, and for several TV programmes. He's been nominated for one Emmy and spent three years working at DC Comics. He lives in Los Angeles, USA, with his wife and their two sons.

LUCIANO VECCHIO was born in 1982 and currently lives in Buenos Aires, Argentina. With experience in illustration, animation and comics, his works have been published in the UK, Spain, USA, France and Argentina. His credits include *Ben 10* (DC Comics), *Cruel Thing* (Norma), *Unseen Tribe* (Zuda Comics) and *Sentinels* (Drumfish Productions).

GLOSSARY

balcony platform with railings on the outside of a building, usually on an upper level

electromagnet magnet formed when electricity flows through a coil of wire

gangplank short bridge or piece of wood used for walking on to and off of a ship

grimaced made a facial expression that indicates a negative reaction to something

hijacking taking illegal control of a ship, plane or other vehicle

hull frame or body of a boat or ship

mesmerized hypnotized or brainwashed

miserable sad, unhappy or dejected

nullified made something useless or cancelled out something

proper right or suitable for a given occasion

DISCUSSION QUESTIONS

1. Batman has his Batarangs. Mr Freeze has his cold gun. Poison Ivy has her toxic plants and pollens. Which weapon do you think is the best? Discuss your answer.

2. Batman's sharp senses help him out in this book. Find a few examples in the story where Batman puts his detective skills to use.

3. This book has ten illustrations. Which one is your favourite? Why?

WRITING PROMPTS

1. Batman counts on Alfred to help him out when the going gets tough. Who do you count on to help you? Who counts on you? Write about your helpful experiences.

2. The ship in this book has a pool, a bowling alley and lots of other fun stuff. Write a few paragraphs about your dream ship, then draw a picture of it.

3. Write a short story where Batman faces off against two super-villains. Which criminals does he fight? How does he manage to defeat them? Write about it.

LOOK FOR MORE

THE DARK KNIGHT

DANGER ON DECK!

SONNEBORN · VECCHIO

BATMAN UNDERCOVER

WEISSBORN · VECCHIO

THE PENGUIN'S CRIME WAVE

SUTTON · VECCHIO

THE BLACK MASQUERADE

TULIEN · VECCHIO